TIMMY AND THE UNICORN

Inger Margaret Foster

Illustrated by Cathlyn A. Driscoll

Text Copyright
2022 by Inger Margaret Foster

Illustration Copyright
2022 by Cathlyn A. Driscoll

Edited by JMG, Inc.
ISBN: 9798839881150
Fiction. Children. Fantasy. Magic.

For Nolan

May You Always
Believe in
Magic

This Book Belongs to:

_____

I'm not sure just where I am
Why am I so soggy?
I really am so confused
And my head feels foggy

My human friend named Mandy
Said she'd be back by noon
She put me here near the fence
I'm sure she'll be here soon

I know how much she loves me
We always like to play
We're together all the time
She holds me tight all day

I don't have much of a choice
I guess I'll have to wait
I really am just a toy
This all must be my fate

But wait! I hear somebody
It's Mandy I am sure
I knew she'd come back for me
But no! It isn't her!

A white horse has come instead
Wait, what on earth is that?
There is something on its head
Is that a party hat?

When the creature moved again
Then I could clearly see
That's not a hat, it's a horn!
It's pointing right at me!

Bowing down to get real close
The horn then tapped my head
Colors sparkled all around
White, green and golden red

My neck became all tingly
The same thing with my knees
My four legs and neck had grown
So tall I touch the trees!

Welcome, Timmy. The mare said
I'm much more than a horse
This horn on my head makes me
A unicorn of course!

I hope that you'll be happy
To be part of the space
In this land of miracles
A special magic place

I made you a real giraffe
Who's ready to explore
We'll head out in just a bit
But wait there's something more!

There's one last thing that you'll need
To make things feel alright
Close your eyes and wait for it!
Be sure to hold on tight!

The next strange thing that happened
Rose up from deep within
First it rumbled in my throat
Then underneath my chin

What do you mean? I then said
But stopped myself in shock
I wasn't only taller
Now I could also talk!

The unicorn said to me
You're capable of speech
You can also think and move
It's all within your reach!

Now carefully, follow me
And I will show you how
One foot here and then the next
That's it! You're walking now!

Partly scared yet also thrilled
I followed right behind
Thinking thoughts I now could speak
I wonder what we'll find?

Turning back to answer me
The unicorn then said
I'm sure you have more questions
But soon it's time for bed

There's a path to guide our way
Through woods so dark and deep
We'll find you a special place
That's safe for you to sleep

Giraffes live in Africa
And other places, too
But not in America
Unless they're in a zoo

You'd cause a great big problem
If you're seen running free
Here is not your habitat
We'll hide you near a tree

In two weeks we'll meet again
Til then just run and play
After that you'll have to choose
To go back or to stay

But now I must leave you here
We'll talk again real soon
Sleep tight, sweet dreams my new friend
Sleep well beneath the moon

As the sun rose in the sky
A song rang in my ear
When I opened up my eyes
A yellow bird appeared

I'm Goldie, a pine warbler
I'm here for you today
Trillium asked if I could help
You try to find your way

I said it's nice to meet you
But I wish that I knew
Why I'm here and what I am
Supposed to really do

Why Timmy you are here now
Because it is your turn
To have the chance to be real
There's much for you to learn

But first, you must hide quickly
Behind this big oak tree
Cars are coming down the road
You're quite the sight to see!

I tucked myself in the leaves
But even though I tried
It became too obvious
I was too tall to hide

Thankfully the passengers
Did not look way up high
If they had they would have seen
My head up near the sky!

I think they're gone, said Goldie
Whispering in my ear
Let's leave right now on our search
Let's take this path right here

Settling in between my horns
She led us on our quest
I think she felt right at home
My head was like her nest!

Roaming through the fields for days
Was fun at first but then
I realized that I missed
What I had way back when

I asked her if we could look
From near and far beyond
To find the place I once knew
The farm with field and pond

Before I knew what happened
A clearing was in sight
A giant field lay ahead
At first it all seemed right

Indeed it was familiar
It was the farm next door
Next to where I once had lived
Way back in the before

Look! Someone's in the distance
I know who it might be
But what is that she's holding?
Is that a stuffed bunny?

I do think I remember
She used to hold *me* tight!
She found something else I guess
This doesn't feel quite right

How has she forgotten me?
She used to be my friend
But then again it was *me*
Who left her in the end

There, there, my friend, said Goldie.
It all will be okay
With her wing so tenderly
She brushed my tears away

Worry not, because you are
Now right where you belong
You will know just what to do
It will not take too long

It's time for me to go now
There's more for you in store
I'll see you in the after
Or back in the before

Perching on my nose she placed
A bird-kiss on my face
In a flash she disappeared
Then Trillium took her place

Trillium said, your time is up
You're back where you began
Two weeks have passed and it's time
Decide now, if you can

But I can wait one more day
The choice is up to you
Stay like this or if you wish
Go back to what you knew

We'll go look in on Mandy
Much later on to see
It might help you to decide
Just where you want to be

As the sun set in the west
The sky was all aglow
Trillium climbed up on my back
And I stood on tip toe

While peeking in the window
We could now clearly see
Mandy tucked into her bed
And holding her bunny

I thought that she had a smile
Upon her little face
Then I looked again real hard
To be sure, just in case

As soon as I saw the tears
Escaping from her eye
I knew what I had to do
I couldn't watch her cry

The choice was really easy
I know now how I feel
Her love for me means so much
Much more than being real

Before I could say a word
It happened in a blink
In a flash, we both fell down
Back to before I think

Just as it did weeks ago
The magic worked once more
I'm no longer tall or real
I'm like I was before

I'm glad I'm home with Mandy
Just like we always were
I had fun being real but
I'm happier with her

We left two more pages especially for you

Inger Margaret Foster
Author

Born in Montreal, Quebec, Inger and her family immigrated to the United States in the early 1960's. Growing up in Ramsey, New Jersey, she attended Ramsey High School, where she developed her love for both writing and art. As an undergrad art major at William Paterson University, she later earned her Masters in Visual Arts, with concentrations in English and Education. Inger has worked as a classroom teacher, art teacher, sales rep and author.

Inger is married and living in New England. She is the mother of three amazing adult children, two wonderful daughters-in-law and is grandmother to one adorable little boy!

Cathlyn A. Driscoll
Illustrator

As a young girl, Cathlyn moved from Bowie, Maryland to Ramsey, New Jersey. She holds a B.A. Degree in Theater (Television Production) from Rutgers University and an Associate's of Applied Science in Graphic Design from Sussex County Community College in New Jersey. As an award winning web/graphic/multimedia designer, Cathlyn has held many positions in the art world: adjunct professor, associate art director, videotape operator and photographer. In addition to running her own business, Happigal Art, Cathlyn is on the board of directors at Frederick Franck's Pacem in Terris Museum, in Warwick, NY.

Cathlyn is married and living in New Jersey. She has two wonderful, talented sons and a lovely daughter-in-law.

Other books written by
Inger Margaret Foster and
Illustrated by Cathlyn A. Driscoll

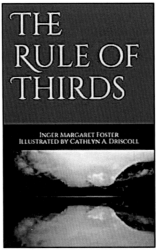

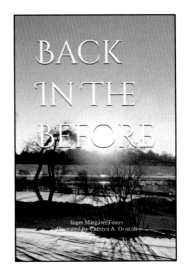

Made in United States
North Haven, CT
12 November 2022

26631242R00022